The Calling of The Heart

Poems Inspired by the Whispering of Each Month

Barry Hunt

Copyright © 2023 Barry Hunt

All rights reserved. This book or any portion thereof may not be reproduced or used in any manner whatsoever without the express written permission of the author except for the use of brief quotations embodied in critical articles and reviews.

All inquiries and permission should be addressed to Barry Hunt: barryrhunt@gmail.com

The Calling of The Heart
Poems Inspired by the Whispering of Each Month
1st Edition

Cover Photo: Barry Hunt

Introduction

The heart is always calling us
to listen intently as the seasons turn,
listen intently
through the wheel of the year,
listen intently
as each month whispers
our divine purpose.

When reading these poems,
I invite you to find that place
where you can listen intently,
that place
where all things stand still
and you can feel
the whispering of each month.

Listening intently
is the path to forgiveness,
empathy and compassion,
the path to seeing ourselves in each other.
Listen now, listen intently
as each month whispers
our divine purpose.

May these poems
find a home
in your heart

Love & blessings

Barry

December: The Calling to Be Still

The days grow shorter
as we approach the Winter Solstice
and then they pause
as the earth tilts on its axis.

We gather at this time to reflect on
the sacred art of pausing,
The Calling to Be Still,
and how it can transform our lives.

Reflect now
on how taking time to be still
is an opportunity to transform
the way we see.

This Is When It Begins

A brilliant star in the night sky,
a brilliant star calling.
I remember now
the dream of a child,
I remember now
the dream of this moment.
I feel it in my heart,
the life I have been longing,
I feel it in my bones,
this is when it begins.

Even the Falling Snow

It can happen any moment,
something that can make you pause,
something that can make you fall
       e reverie of stillness.

           lling snow,
          o lightly,
           pause.
           lake,
          g robe,
          ake,
           t opens your heart
           f stillness.

A Moment When I See

For nine days in December
the people of the pueblo
gather at dusk to welcome
Our Lady of Guadalupe.

They gather at dusk to wait
with candles in their hands
and candles in their hearts
for the maiden they chose
to wear the mantle of Guadalupe.

There is a moment at dusk
when the rays of lingering light
are like corn silk,
a moment when I see
her shimmering mantle
and the crowd parting
as she walks to the pickup truck
that would carry her
to the town plaza,
a moment when I see
her looking at us
with candles in our hands
and candles in our hearts,
looking at us
with humility and compassion,
looking at us
with the eyes of Our Lady of Guadalupe.

January: The Calling to Dream

When the ground is covered with snow
draw your attention inward;
this is the time to dream
the Dream of Spirit Bear.

This is the time to dream
of how everything is sacred,
how everything has a role,
a place on the totem.

Reflect now
on what we hold sacred
and carve it into our life
so we may take our place.

This Is the Time to Dream

I am speaking for the mountains
all covered in snow,
I am speaking for the mountains
when I say,
this is the time to dream.

This is the time to dream
of what might be
when the snow melts
and the streams flow
and all your dreams unfold
like spring flowers.

Listen to the mountains calling,
listen to the mountains
as they say,
this is the time to dream.

The Dream of Spirit Bear

Only on a clear day
when hope is resplendent
upon the Olympic range
and swells across the strait
of Juan de Fuca,
only on a clear day
will the Garry Oak crones
whisper of it,
a time when man stood
as spirit bear
in the sacred circle
with eagle, salmon and raven.

Only on a clear day
when hope is resplendent
on the Olympic range
and swells across the strait
of Juan de Fuca,
only on a clear day
will the Garry Oak crones
whisper of it,
the dream of spirit bear,
how all things are sacred,
how all things have a role
and place in the sacred circle
and how the earth
is our shared home.

Murmurations

When I see swooping starlings
flying in murmurations,
flying in patterns
so complex,
so intricate,
yet never collide;
when I see them
come together
and fly as one,
I am mesmerized
and I wonder
how they do it!

I wonder
if they come together
in a way
we have yet to comprehend.
I wonder
if it might have something to do
with seeing ourselves
in each other,
seeing ourselves as one
and I wonder
if we might ever
fly like starlings!

February: The Calling of Inspiration

Deep within
this dream of Winter
sense something stirring,
the first stirring of Spring.

Sense this impulse
stirring in everything,
a fullness calling,
an invitation of Light.

Reflect now
on The Calling of Inspiration
and how it is like
the first stirring of Spring.

This Stirring Within

Deep within
this dream of Winter
I sense something stirring,
an impulse to wake,
an impulse to rise,
to reveal all that I am.

I welcome it
and how it makes me feel
more alive
and happy to be alive,
aligned with the rhythms
all round me.

I see it
in the first stirring of spring,
I see it in the snowdrop
and I feel how it must feel
with the tender touch
of rising light.

I see this impulse in everything,
an impulse to wake,
an impulse to rise
and turn towards something more,
a fullness calling,
an invitation of light.

The First Signs of Spring

When you look
for the first signs of Spring,
what will it be,
perhaps the white petals
of Compassion?

The Song of the Moon

Listen with all your heart
to the song of the moon.
Listen as she sings
of what is vital
to wake our dreams.
She sings of the soil
where we lay our dreams
and how to ready the soil,
to till and turn the soil,
to dig deep into the earth,
to find what is vital.
She sings of our hearts
and how they are the soil
where we lay our dreams
and how to ready the soil,
to till and turn the soil,
to dig deep into our hearts,
to find what is vital,
the rich, moist matter
of what is vital.
Listen with all your heart
to the song of the moon.
Listen as she sings
of what is vital
to wake our dreams.

March: The Calling to Wake

When the Wheel of the Year
turns to Spring,
all that was sleeping
begins to wake.

Now the daffodil
begins to trumpet
and we join our voice
with the thousand voices of praise.

Reflect now
on how all things wake
and the nature
of Alchemy.

Today

Today,
when the rest of the world,
and meaning and purpose,
seem so far away,
the song birds are welcoming a new day.

Today,
the song birds helped me realize
that only we can give this day,
meaning and purpose.

Perhaps it may be calling
or texting someone
we have not connected with for some time
to see if they are okay,
to let them know
we are thinking of them.

Perhaps it may be starting a new project,
an exercise program,
yoga or meditation,
a journal or memoir,
spring cleaning.

There is always something
we have been meaning to do,
something we have put off for another day
because we have been too busy,

something else has been more important.

Today,
we can do it.
Today,
we can give this day
meaning and purpose.

Today,
we can join our voice
with the song birds
welcoming a new day.

Today,
I choose to wash the leaves
of the philodendron in the carport.
They are covered with dust from the road.
I had put it off for another day
because I had been too busy,
something else had been more important.

Today,
I hold each leaf
in the palm of my hand
and with my other hand
I wipe each leaf tenderly.

The leaves remind me
of the hands of a child.
I remember the hands of my daughter.

I remember wiping her hands
after she had been playing in the yard.
I remember how much I loved caring for her.
I remember how happy I felt
wiping her hands.

And I think of all the children in the world,
and all the things growing,
all the things that need our care,
all the things that give life
meaning and purpose.

The Love of Light in All Things Growing

Each day I see it more clearly
this longing we have
for the touch of light.
I see it quivering
in all things growing.
I see it
in the pilgrim branch
offering a drop of dew,
offering it
for the touch of light.

The Thousand Voices of Praise

On this brilliant morning
as I stand on the bridge
overlooking the murmuring brook,
I hear the heart of the world
singing with praise,
singing even more fervently,
now that we realize
how precious our world is.

On this brilliant morning
as I stand on the bridge
overlooking the murmuring brook,
I hear the sighing mist
rising from the pond,
the echoing strains
of the trumpeter swan,
and in a distant field,
glistening horses,
their hair singing in the morning light.

Let this be the morning
to stand on the bridge
overlooking the murmuring brook
and hear the heart of the world
singing with praise.
Let this be the morning
to join our voices
with the thousand voices of praise.

April: The Calling of Love

Hildegaard von Begin
said that Love
was the Greening Power of God,
the vibrancy of Spring.

She said that Spring
is an invitation
to welcome
the greening power of Love.

Reflect now
on The Calling of Love
and how we might welcome it
into our hearts and lives.

The Tango of Beginning

Let us begin
as if
there is always
a beginning,
heart to heart,
estilo milonguero,
as we stride
across the floor
and with a flourish
stride back once more
and you look into my eyes
as if
for the first time,
even though
it has always been
la vay y ven,
the to and fro,
la ocho,
the tango of beginning.

The Milk of Life

If you want to know
what love is
and how to find it
ask one who knows,
ask a mother.
She will say
love is the milk of life.
She will say
you can find it
by giving all that you are.
She will say
you can see it
in the setting sun,
giving all that it is
in that precious moment.
She will say
this is the truth you seek,
this is the path to follow,
giving all that you are
in every precious moment.

I Am Watching as if I Was the Moon

I am watching
the ebb and flow,
the wave rising
and then receding.
I am watching
as if I was the moon,
I am watching
as if I had a prayer.

I am invoking
fire and air,
earth, water and ether,
I am invoking
all the elements
that shape our world,
I am invoking them
to shape a world of love.

I am waiting
for the first signs,
the snowdrop
and the robin's song,
I am waiting
for it to be revealed,
a world where love
is the purpose in all we do.

May: The Calling of Wonder

In Spanish,
the word for Wonder
is *Encantamiento*.
I like to think of it as luminescence.

It is the stars in the heavens
and the stars in the sea,
the crystals of light
all around us.

Reflect now
on The Calling of Wonder
and how we might welcome
Wonder into our lives.

There is Wonder in Every Precious Moment

If I could pinch this moment
between my thumb and forefinger,
this precious moment
when the sun holds the sea
in golden splendour,
I would put this moment
in a locket
to rest upon your heart.

This world is such a busy place.
We never seem to have a precious moment
when we can hold each other
in golden splendour
and in our most tender voice
whisper what the sun
and the sea whisper
in that precious moment.

Encantamiento

Encantamiento
is all around us
calling us from slumber.

Encantamiento
is luminescence,
it is the stars in the heavens
and the stars in the sea,
the crystals of light
all around us
calling us from slumber.

You can see it in San Pancho
on Friday nights
when there is music
in the street.
You can see the crystals of light
sparkling on faces
of people who stop to listen,
sparkling on faces
of people dancing in the street
or tapping their hips
to the heartbeat of
encantamiento.

From early light,
when the song birds are calling
the sun from slumber,

to twilight,
when the golden light
and the purple light
dance over the bay,
Encantamiento
is all around us
calling us from slumber.

The Long Roll of the Snare Drum

I want to rise and shine,
to be the first in line
to see the majorette
and the baton
as she tosses it
high into the air.
Holding my breath
with the long roll
of the snare drum,
this life is too precious
to miss a moment!

June: The Calling of The Sacred Marriage

Father Sky
and Mother Earth
are at the peak of their energies
at the time of the Summer Solstice.

When they come together as One
we celebrate the Sacred Union
of the Divine Masculine
and Divine Feminine.

Reflect now
on The Calling of the Sacred Marriage
and what it means in our lives,
how we welcome and nourish it.

The Sacred Union

When every heart beat
is my sacred vow
and every breath
an elixir
transmuting all that I am
into gold,
then every bird singing,
every flower blooming,
every mountain peak
and river flowing,
every sunrise
and sunset
is illumined,
a blessed child of this union.

This Life is Your Wedding Gown

This life is your wedding gown.
Come to this moment
as if it is the Ceremony.
Come to this moment
with flowers in your hair,
with flowers in your hand.

Offer yourself completely
to the divinity
of who you truly are.
Offer yourself completely
to the One who has waited
through all these lifetimes.

Wear your life
as if every moment
is the Ceremony.
Come to this moment
with flowers in your hair,
with flowers in your hand.

My Heart is Hopelessly in Love with Everything

My heart is hopelessly in love
with everything.
It is singing
like a song bird at dawn,
singing to the hearts
in everything,
everything grazing
on the hillsides
and in the meadows,
everything swimming
in the ocean
and the mountain stream.

My heart is singing
to the hearts in everything,
the trees yearning for the sun,
the chalices of hibiscus
filled with the nectar of love,
the honey bees
and the hummingbirds
thirsting for the nectar of love.

There is thirsting
and yearning
and singing
in the hearts of everything
and when this thirsting

and yearning
and singing
is overflowing,
there is dancing,
dancing in the hearts of everything.

July: The Calling of Compassion

As the Seasons turn
through the Wheel of the Year
they remind us
of the evolving nature of Love.

When we have all we could ever want,
when our hearts are overflowing,
then Compassion
flows through our lives.

Reflect now
on The Calling of Compassion
and how it flows through our lives
and the world around us.

May All We Do be Shaped Like Compassion

The Parota tree stands tall and still
and offers its branches as shelter
for all who need shelter.
It is called the listening tree
because its seeds pods
are shaped like ears.

May we be like the listening tree.
may we stand tall and still
and offer shelter
for all who need shelter
and may all we do
be shaped like compassion.

Listen

Now that there are no demands
on me or my time
I am learning to walk
without purpose.

I am learning to walk
as fast or slow as I wish
and to stop
whenever something speaks to me
in a way that draws me near.

It might be the birds singing
somewhere in the trees.
It might be the sun
breaking through the clouds
and streaming over the fields
or the cows
grazing in the fields,
the mothers looking up
watchful of their calves.
the calves without a care
stretching their heads
through the barbed wire
for the tall grass just within reach.

There is a tree I pass on my morning walk.
All the leaves have fallen
and only the seed pods remain.

They are shaped like ears
as if they are asking me to listen,
to listen in a way
that sends roots deep into this moment.

When I listen in this way
I feel my branches stretching
as far as I can see.
I feel the birds perching
on my branches
and their song
coursing through me
like sap from my deepest roots
to my tallest branches
and I feel the warmth
of their song
streaming over my fields
and I taste the sweetness
of their song
in the tall grass just within reach.

Just Trying to Find Our Way

I always thought of him
as the town drunk
singing to the stars
while staggering down the street,
singing to the stars
about whatever demons
were haunting him.
So I was surprised
to see him there
wearing his best
cowboy boots and hat
with a guitar and harmonica
backing up the main singer.
And I realized then
that I was too quick to judge.
He really wasn't
any different than me,
just trying to find his way.
We all have dark nights
singing to whatever stars will listen.

August: The Calling of Gratitude

The golden fields of grain
swaying gently
under the August light
reminds us that all is well.

The Celtic celebration of Lammas,
the grain harvest,
the first harvest of the season,
reminds us of all that Nature provides.

Reflect now
on The Calling of Gratitude
and the role
that Gratitude has in our lives.

Queen Anne's Lace

When we open our hearts
life can be like a meadow
filled with Queen Anne's Lace,
a meadow of delicate discoveries
towering far above
what we may have expected.

When we open our hearts
an umbel
of delicate discoveries,
an inflorescence
of stems, stalks and flowers,
springs into bloom.

When we open our hearts
life can be like a meadow
filled with Queens Anne's Lace
where the baskets
of butterflies and bees
carry delicate discoveries.

These are the Days Worth Picking

These are the days
worth picking
when the fingers
of the early morning sun
reach through the treetops
for what is ripe.

These are the days
worth picking
when the light reaches
through the treetops
and you no longer can hide
all you have become.

An Empty Fullness

There is always a moment
after the parade down main street,
the last beat
of the snare and the bass drum,
there is always a moment,
an empty fullness,
before we breathe again.

September: The Calling of Reflection

This is the time
when we reap
what we have sown,
a time of reflection.

The Fall Equinox
marks the second harvest
of the Autumn season,
the Fruit Harvest.

Reflect now
on The Fruit Harvest
and the role
that Reflection has in our lives.

All is Ripe

There comes a moment
in the late days of summer
when a golden contentment
falls upon us,
a moment
before we celebrate,
a moment when we realize
all is ripe.

The Remembering

It all happened so quickly,
the touch of youth
fallen from my embrace,
but each day now
the bright parade of leaves
beckons me
to a joy and peace
that comes with accepting
what will be.

The Glacial Grinding of Bedrock

The First People are the soil of this land,
they are the rock flour
from the glacial grinding of bedrock,
they are the silt suspended in the water
and the turquoise colour of these lakes
when the sun shines upon them.

They have weathered
the slow glacial grind.
Climb the Enderby Cliffs,
the Skaha Bluffs,
the *nʕaylintn* (nye-lin-tin)
to see what they have seen.

They are our elders, our sagebrush,
they show us how to honour the four directions
and the four sacred medicines,
tobacco, cedar, sage and sweetgrass.
They show us how to honour the earth
and all the beings who live here.

When you stand upon the mountaintop
and you listen with your heart,
when you listen to the wind
and the stories in the wind,
it will be their voice you hear,
the glacial grinding of bedrock.

October: The Calling of Home

When the work of Spring
and summer are done,
return to hearth and home
to share the bounty.

This life is such a grand
and noble quest,
to know who we are
and the nature of this world.

Reflect now
on The Calling of Home
and the role that home
has in our lives.

Home is as Close to You as Breathing

That place where you feel at ease,
at peace with yourself and the world,
not troubled by what you have done
or what you have yet to do,
let's call that place home.

You may feel
that you have wandered far from home.
that you have lost your way,
but home has never left you.
It is as close to you as breathing.

Turn your attention there,
to the blessing of breath.
Breathe in
as if you were a wave
rolling into shore.

Now let it go,
leave it on the shore,
what you have done
and what you have yet to do
as if you were a wave coming home.

When You Lean Over the Stream of Your Life

When you lean over
the stream of your life
as tenderly
as a cedar bough,
see all your efforts
guiding you back
to where they began.
Like the salmon running,
see all your efforts
guiding you home.

Everything is a Centering Prayer

When we sacrifice our natural world
on the cross of our ambitions,
when we settle our affairs
with the loudest voice,
when the seeds of compassion
lie dormant in our hearts,
then we have lost our center
and must find our way there.

It may be a way of letting go,
it may be a way of connecting
or a way of being still.
It may be calling upon
the energies of where we are,
the energies of the earth,
the air and water.
It may be calling upon our ancestors,
it may be calling upon the children
yet to come,
calling them to this moment,
calling them with our way of letting go,
calling them with our way of connecting
or our way of being still.

Everything is a way there,
everything is a centering prayer,
how we are in this moment,

how we dance
and how we are still,
how we are with one another
and how we are with all beings,
how we are with the earth,
the air and water,
everything is a way there,
everything is a centering prayer.

November: The Calling to Let Go

November is the long, cold walk
to the still time of the year,
when we hold close
what we hold dear.

It is the time
to let go
of what we no longer need,
to be the hollow reed.

Reflect now
on The Calling to Let Go,
and the role that letting go
has in our lives.

Dance Madly in Naked Delight

As the valiant rays
take their bow
and the forest nymphs
let go their gowns
to dance madly
in naked delight,
I will dance with them
while the light still lingers,
I will dance with them,
dance madly
in naked delight.

The Old Man and the Well

Early each morning
the old man lowers his bucket
into the well.
He can feel the bucket fill
by the pull on the rope.

He remembers the snow melting
and buds on branches.
He remembers planting seeds
in the rich, dark soil.
He remembers the warmth of summer
and caring for the garden.
He remembers the harvest
and the bounty of the table.
He remembers each season
and the joy of each one.

When I Take That Next Step

In the late afternoon light
the bleached stalks of maize,
once so tall and proud,
make me think of that next step.

I know we don't talk about it,
but I don't know why
for it is a step
we all must take.

I remember my sister calling
to say the time is near
and flying out with my wife.
I remember the four of us,
my sister and I,
her husband and my wife,
there with my father
before his next step.

He did not believe in God
but he had a dream
on one of those last nights,
sitting on the bank of a stream
under the shade of a tree
on a warm summer day,
sitting contentedly
as the stream passed by.

No insurance is provided on

C. Uballe-Johnson
Customer Signature

_____
Customer Signature

Revised: 04/08

I remember his last breath
and waiting for the next breath
that never came.
I remember sitting in silence
to give his soul time
and then telling him
we would be fine,
he could leave us now.

When my time is near
I like to think
that I will have friends
and family close,
a chance to say goodbye,
to know they are well
before I turn away
to take that next step.

Manufactured by Amazon.ca
Bolton, ON

34601856R00037